FEB 2 5 2004

Dear Parents,

Welcome to the Scholastic Reader series. We have taken over 80 years of experience with teachers, parents, and children and put it into a program that is designed to match your child's interests and skills.

Level 1—Short sentences and stories made up of words kids can sound out using their phonics skills and words that are important to remember.

Level 2—Longer sentences and stories with words kids need to know and new "big" words that they will want to know.

Level 3—From sentences to paragraphs to longer stories, these books have large "chunks" of texts and are made up of a rich vocabulary.

Level 4—First chapter books with more words and fewer pictures.

It is important that children learn to read well enough to succeed in school and beyond. Here are ideas for reading this book with your child:

- Look at the book together. Encourage your child to read the title and make a prediction about the story.
- Read the book together. Encourage your child to sound out words when appropriate. When your child struggles, you can help by providing the word.
- Encourage your child to retell the story. This is a great way to check for comprehension.
- Have your child take the fluency test on the last page to check progress.

Scholastic Readers are designed to support your child's efforts to learn how to read at every age and every stage. Enjoy helping your child learn to read and love to read.

> —**Francie Alexander**
> Chief Education Officer
> Scholastic Education

TM

BY **B.J. JAMES**
ILLUSTRATED BY **CHRIS DEMAREST**

For Sahve
—B.J.J.

For Rich, Scott, & Kim
—C.D.

Text copyright © 2003 by Brian Masino.
Illustrations copyright © 2003 by Chris Demarest.
All rights reserved. Published by Scholastic Inc.
SCHOLASTIC, CARTWHEEL BOOKS, and associated logos are trademarks and/or registered trademarks of Scholastic Inc.

Library of Congress Cataloging-in-Publication Data
James, B.J.
  Supertwins and Tooth Trouble / by B.J. James; illustrated by Chris Demarest.
    p. cm. — (Scholastic Reader—Level 2) "Cartwheel Books."
Summary: Twin superheroes Timmy and Tabby fly off in pursuit of a thief when the lost teeth they have placed under their pillows disappear and no money replaces them.
  ISBN 0-439-46624-5 (pbk. : alk. paper)
    [1. Heroes—Fiction. 2. Twins—Fiction. 3. Brothers and sisters—Fiction. 4. Robbers and outlaws—Fiction. 5. Teeth—Fiction. 6. Tooth Fairy—Fiction.] I. Demarest, Chris L., ill. II. Title. III. Series.
PZ7.J153585 Su 2003
[Fic]—dc21
2002009312   CIP

12 11 10 9 8 7 6 5 4 3 2 1   03 04 05 06 07
Printed in the U.S.A. 23 • First printing, May 2003

Scholastic Reader — Level 2

SCHOLASTIC INC.

New York Toronto London Auckland Sydney
Mexico City New Delhi Hong Kong Buenos Aires

Chapter 1

I lost my front tooth.
And Tabby lost hers!

"Put your teeth under your pillow," said Mom.
"The Tooth Fairy will take your teeth. She will pay you money for them."

I wonder if we will get more money because our teeth are super teeth.

We went to sleep.

"The Tooth Fairy stole our teeth!"
Tabby said. "And she didn't
give us any money!"
Tabby was really, really, really MAD!

I didn't think the Tooth Fairy
had stolen our teeth.
"Maybe a thief took our teeth,"
I said.
"No. It was the Tooth Fairy!"
Tabby said.
But we didn't have time to fight.
It was time to go to school.

Chapter 2

At bedtime, Tabby and
I snuck out.
We were super quiet.

We flew to Kara's house.
Tabby won.
I said we weren't racing.

I snuck up to the window.
Superheroes have to be sneaky!
I peeked.
Kara was asleep.
The Tooth Fairy was not there yet.

"Look!" I shouted.
"Don't shout!" Tabby whispered.
I forgot. We needed to be quiet.

We saw the Tooth Fairy
tiptoe into Kara's room.

Tabby peeked in the window.
The Tooth Bandit peeked out.

"That's not the Tooth Fairy!" Tabby yelled.
"Let's get him!"

The Tooth Bandit ran away.

IN THE TOOTH CAVE...

the Tooth Fairy was in a cage.
The Tooth Bandit was laughing.
He had every kid's tooth!
He had every kid's dollar!

Luckily, Tabby can see through rocks.
The Tooth Bandit had a super-big machine.
It could turn teeth into gold!

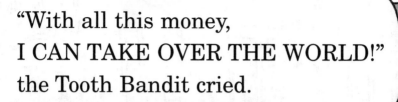

"With all this money, I CAN TAKE OVER THE WORLD!" the Tooth Bandit cried.

Then . .

Tabby and I smashed through the wall!

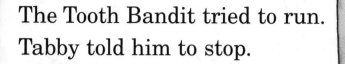

The Tooth Bandit tried to run.
Tabby told him to stop.

I flew as fast as lightning.
I reached the cage.
I tried to pick it up.
But it was very heavy.
I had to use all my super strength!
I did it!

The Tooth Bandit tried to get away.
But Tabby tripped him.
He fell down.

Then . . .

CRASH!

I dropped the cage on him.
Finally, he was where he belonged—
behind bars!

"Let me out!" he cried.
"No way!" I said. "You are staying
here for a long, long, long time!"
"Yes," Tabby said. "AND, I want my dollar!"

Chapter 3

"Thank you! Thank you!"
cried the Tooth Fairy.
The Tooth Fairy was free.
She gave me a hug.
She gave Tabby a hug, too.
She gave Tabby a kiss.
She gave me a kiss, too.
YUCK!

The Tooth Fairy looked around.
"How will I get all this money
to all the kids?" she asked.
"We will help!" Tabby and I shouted.

All night long, we put dollars under pillows.

I put a dollar under Tabby's pillow. Then we went to bed.

I told Tabby to tuck in her cape. She always forgets.

The next day,
Tabby told Kara how we saved the world.
It is supposed to be a secret, but Tabby
always tells.
"There was this tooth bandit.
And Timmy picked up this BIG cage.
And . . ."

"No there wasn't," Kara said.
"Look, I got my dollar!
You two are so silly!"

No one EVER believes a superhero!

Fluency Fun

The words in each list below end in the same sounds.
Read the words in a list.
Read them again.
Read them faster.
Try to read all 15 words in one minute.

gave	bake	dime
save	lake	lime
wave	make	time
brave	take	prime
grave	snake	slime

Look for these words in the story.

under	our	could
quiet	every	

Note to Parents:

According to A *Dictionary of Reading and Related Terms*, fluency is "the ability to read smoothly, easily, and readily with freedom from word-recognition problems." Fluency is necessary for good comprehension and enjoyable reading. The activities on this page include a speed drill and a sight-recognition drill. Speed drills build fluency because they help students rapidly recognize common syllables and spelling patterns in words, and they're fun! Sight-recognition drills help students smoothly and accurately recognize words. Practice these activities with your child to help him or her become a fluent reader.

—**Wiley Blevins,**
Reading Specialist